This Book
Belongs To

_____

Sesame Workshop Books

ISBN: 0-375-80322-X

www.randomhouse.com/kids/sesame

www.sesamestreet.com

Printed in Italy October 2000 10 9 8 7 6 5 4 3 2 1

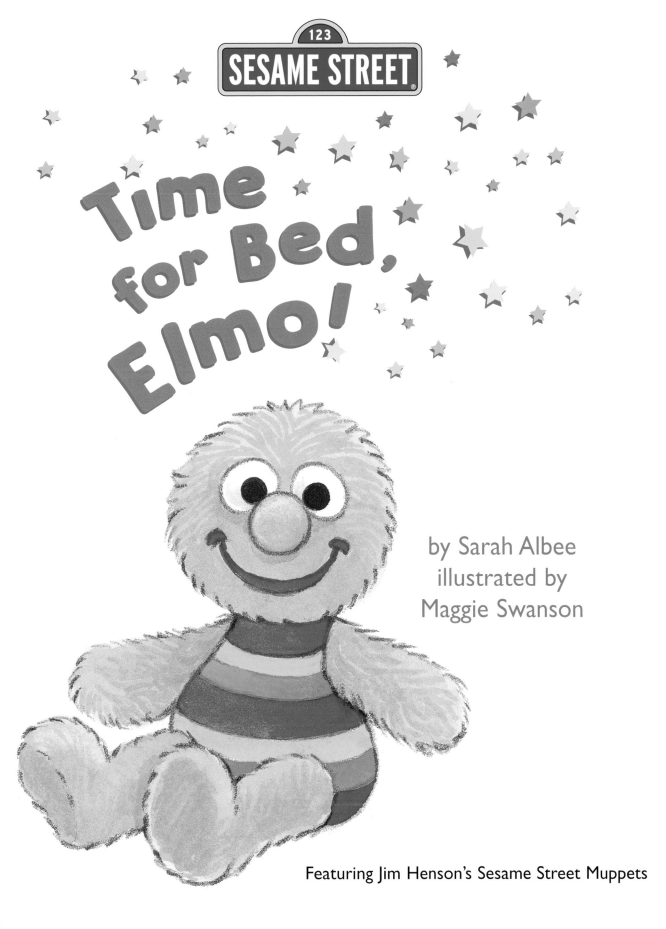

SESAME STREET

Time for Bed, Elmo!

by Sarah Albee
illustrated by
Maggie Swanson

Featuring Jim Henson's Sesame Street Muppets

Elmo's babysitter says, "It's time to
go to bed."
But Elmo needs his pillow plumped and
one more story read!

He has to turn his night-light on and close the closet door.

And he has to put his toys away! He left
them on the floor.

He has to check beneath the bed to see if something's there.

He needs the window open—monsters like
a little air!

He'd better make a potty trip—he just might
need to use it.

And screw the toothpaste cap on tight. He wouldn't want to lose it!

He'll want a cup of water next to him for nighttime sipping.
Uh-oh. It sounds like someone left the bathroom faucet dripping!

Elmo didn't pet the cat!

He didn't feed the fish!

And while he's up, he'll find a star and make a little wish.

He's checking all his boo-boos. Here's a
new one on his knee.
Elmo needs a bandage on it. Do you want
to see?

He'll try the potty yet again—he just might have to go.

He'd better close the window now. It looks
like it might snow.

He has to straighten up the books and stack the building blocks.
And find that missing puzzle piece and pick up all his socks.

Maybe he'll get sleepy if he tries some exercise! "Elmo!" calls the babysitter. "Time to close your eyes!"

"Elmo, dear," the sitter calls, "now not another peep!"
Maybe you can help him out by softly counting sheep.

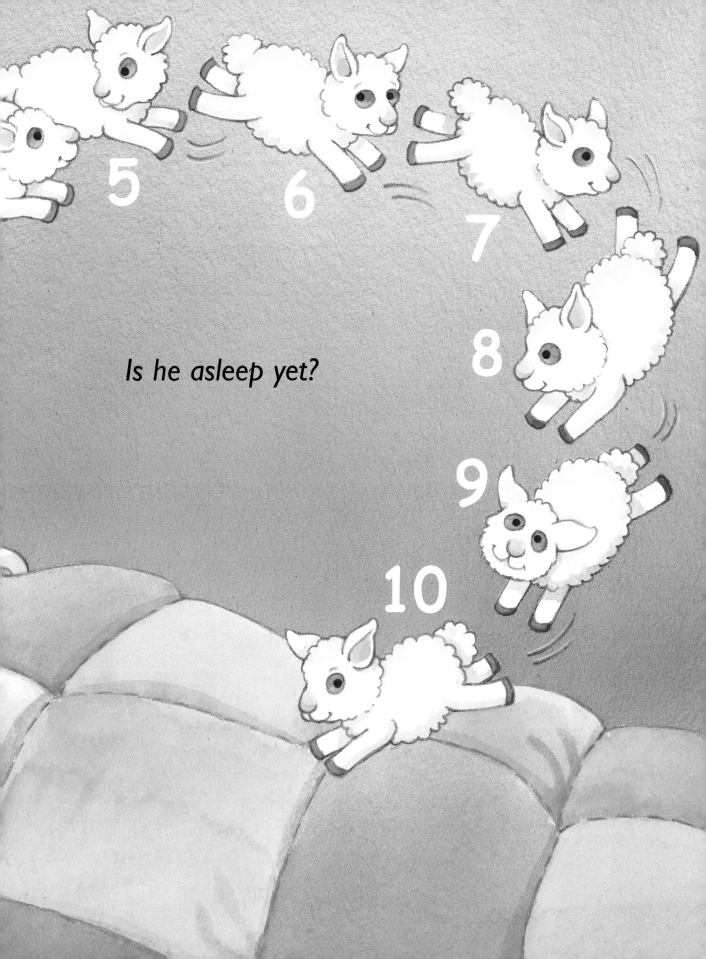

Is he asleep yet?

"Oh, my!" the sitter whispers.
"The monster's sound asleep!"

Good night, Elmo.